©1989
Text by Robert Priest
Illustrations by Katherine Helmer

Published in July, 1989 by
Black Moss Press,
1939 Alsace Avenue,
Windsor, Ontario,
Canada N8W 1M5

with the assistance of the
Canada Council and the
Ontario Arts Council.

Black Moss Books are
distributed in Canada and
the United States by:

Firefly Books
250 Sparks Avenue
Willowdale, Ontario
Canada M2H 2S4

All orders should be
directed there.

ISBN 0-88753-196-2
First printing July 1989

Printed in Canada by
The National Press,
Toronto, Ontario

To Ananda Eli
and Daniel
and to all babies everywhere
Special thanks to Allen Booth.

TEN BIG BABIES

POEM BY ROBERT PRIEST
ILLUSTRATIONS BY KATHERINE HELMER

Black Moss Press

There were ten big babies
who wouldn't go to sleep
go to sleep

One sweet song and a little starshine
then there were...

Nine big babies
who wouldn't go to sleep
go to sleep

One long yaaaawn 'cause another couldn't wait
then there were...

Eight big babies
who wouldn't go to sleep
go to sleep

Eight winks, nine winks, ten, eleven
then there were...

Seven tired babies
who wouldn't go to sleep
go to sleep

The old clock in the corner tox and tix
then there were...

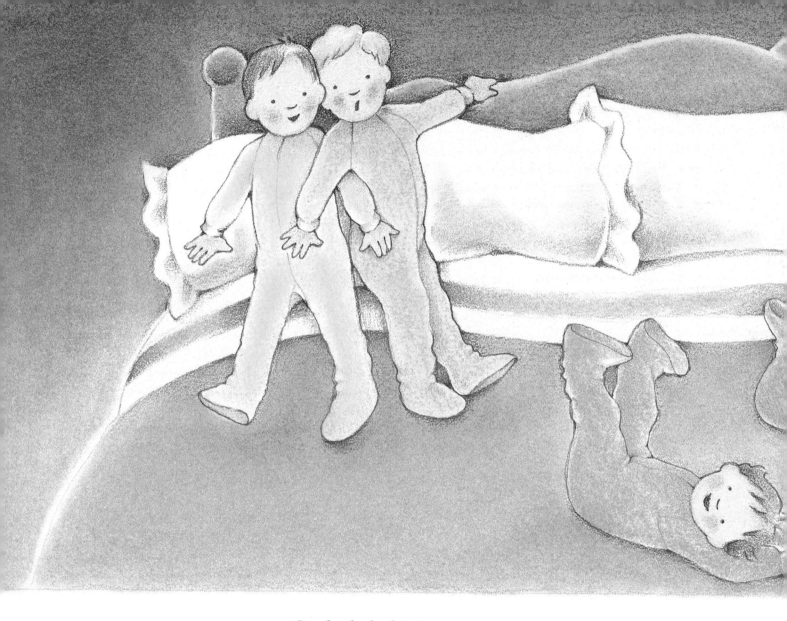

Six little babies
who wouldn't go to sleep
go to sleep

They snore like buzzin' bees in a hive
then there were...

Five big babies
who wouldn't go to sleep
go to sleep

I can't stay awake a second more
then there were...

Four sweet babies
who wouldn't go to sleep
go to sleep

Raindrops on the roof fall gently
then there were...

Three tired babies
who wouldn't go to sleep
go to sleep

Dream of me and I will dream of you
then there were...

Two big babies
who wouldn't go to sleep
go to sleep

Now my song is almost done
now there's only...

One tired baby
about to go to sleep

go to sleep

good night!